Hug Me

Patti Stren

North Winds Press
A Division of Scholastic Canada Ltd.

This book is dedicated to my father, Mr. Maurie Stren

(August 25, 1910–January 2, 1995), a wise and gentle man. And I miss him so.

How could I not mention the remarkable people who have been my source of inspiration and seamless courage: my big brother David (my first publisher and the "quiet genius" navigating my career). With all my love to my mother, Sadie Stren—an archivist and a poet whose writing and kindness simply astound me. Then the extraordinary Cara and Daniel Zacks. (What happened? I turned my head . . . and you grew up so admirably. In loving memory of your grandpa—Mr. Andy Frank.) Tenderly, and in memory of my dear author Jim Friedman, for graciously allowing me to make pictures for his beloved Foy Rin Jin (miss you, J.F.). And to Alice, the Face. And to the magnificent Hanna Teush (wow, you're great!). Sweetness to U, Ann Borins. U2, Bart. To the coolest and sweetest boy, Omar Yasbek. (The mice miss you! Bubba misses you. Me 2!) And in loving memory of Donna Conrad, the most beautiful, elegant and mischievous woman I have ever known. And in loving memory of Dr. Leslie Karp (you are remembered). "Play like champions today"—the Eanellis. Beth Ann, Tommy, Kate Jocee and Monica. And to you, Tom Eanelli, M.D., for putting your heart ♡ on the line. Love to the remarkable Jimmy "Jimmers" Kennedy (hit one out of the ball park for me, will you, Jimmers!). ⌣ Avec tendresse to C*. Love to the Cherniaks—Sharon and Bobby, Rebecca (a writer I admire so and a cutie pie 2!) and of course Aaron. (Archie, you are a one in a million guy! A champ.) Sophie, I think you're fabulous and cool. Schnoodles of hugs to Liam and Stephen McNally (Gramma and Grandpa too!). Love to A & L & S & S Gerber & Elijah & Kaitlin & Nadine (kisses from NYC). To the magical princess on the West Side—Emily McCormack (everything about you is simply wondrous). To the kindest and smartest guy on the planet—James "Grumpy" Freehill (I'm simply crazy for you, Grumpy!). Dozens of dolphin kisses to Judy Messinger (you are "the magic"). Smoocheroonies galore to the boldest and most unique gorgeous babe—Ronnie Heekin (never change, RH). U2, Frank! Oooodles of hugs and kisses to Andreas, Mia, and Juliya Singer and Singer Travel Service. (Rich, you are amazing.) Mona Mon Amour sends kisses to Donald Harrison and Victoria and Mary. xoxoxo. And to MLW (tenderness counts). Kibbings to Heather, Nicky, and Jenna. U2, Doug. (Miss Auntie Doll and Uncle Herman terribly.) Love to Lois Fishman and Henry and especially Neff Law Associates for believing in me. And a million gazillion merci beaucoups, Tanya Mallean and Bill Skrzyniarz (for being my champions—with heart!). And to Howard Beckerman, the one, the only who believed in me over 23 years ago—and remains the one true mensch in town. Kisses, Iris. Admire U, Judge Edra Ferguson (send U hugs). Throwing rainbow kisses to Kim Todd (Original Pictures)—for believing in Emma right from the beginning! And in loving memory of Emma Goldberg, my gramma who talked to me about color and—love. And to the most original young girl—Andrea Wilson (what a ♡ you have!). Clementine kisses to Beth Stewart's fingertips. Hey, CinéGroupe! Big bearhug to Emma's Champion—Adrian Mills (CBC). In loving memory of Ela Moll and hugs to Alanna, Eli, Elysa, Jason and especially to you, my dearest Ruthie. {{{Bathed in color}}} Itsy Duncan looks up, amazed—gushes, a nod and a wink to Michael Sporn for breathing life into Elliot Kravitz, Thelma Claypits, Mona Mon Amour and in fact . . . Itsy. And with both ears, Mona perks up with wonder and listens to the magic of Editor Ed Askinazi. And with all my tenderness to John Cirgliano and family and Gary Senick and parents. And in memory of John Gardner, the writer, a wondrous man who first saw Hug Me and believed in my work. And without a doubt, to John & Patricia Mitrano (my heart tugs every time I look at your daughter's face), and avec tendresse to Charles Pachter—for being my inspiration. And last, and most important, to the love of my life, Dr. Richard F. Cohen (Rich). You are truly the unsung hero. Your kindness and courage move me. And I adore you. Simply flat out adore you, my dearest, darling husband.

National Library of Canada Cataloguing in Publication Data / Stren Patti, 1950- / Hug me / ISBN 0-439-98749-0 / I. Title. /

PS8587.T724H8 2002   jC813'.54   C2001-902695-1   PZ7.S9163Hu 2002a

North Winds Press, a division of Scholastic Canada Ltd., 175 Hillmount Road, Markham, Ontario L6C 1Z7, Canada

6 5 4 3 2 1   Printed and bound in Canada   02 03 04 05

Hug Me

Elliot Kravitz was not like other porcupines, who were quite content having quills and being left alone.

Elliot was not content. He wanted a friend. A friend to talk to, a friend to play with and tell his best secrets to. But mostly, he wanted a friend to hug.

All the porcupines told him, "Hey, Elliot! It's really great having quills!!

"No one bothers us. We always get to be first in line. We never have to share our ice-cream cones. No one ever comes near a porcupine!"

But Elliot liked being with others. He didn't mind sharing his ice cream, even if it was a double-scoop, chocolate-chip cone with sprinkles on top.

Elliot longed for a friend. You see, the one thing he wanted more than anything else in the world was a big, tight... HUG. The other porcupines wouldn't hug him. It's too hard, they said, to hug someone with quills.

So Elliot spent most of his time

hugging telephone poles . . .

parking meters . . .

and traffic lights.

After a while, Elliot got tired of hugging telephone poles, parking meters, and traffic lights. They really didn't make him feel very good.

At night, in bed, Elliot would dream about
having a real friend who would hug back.

One morning, he got out of bed and said,
"Enough is enough. No more hugging parking
meters, traffic lights, and telephone poles. I
want a friend to hug! A friend who will hug
me back!"

Elliot disguised himself as a birthday present. Everyone loves birthday presents. Maybe someone who loved birthday presents would want to be his friend.

At Christmastime, Elliot put lights around each quill and rented himself out as the first walking Christmas tree.

Everyone loved to look at him, but no one ever
wanted to hug him.

Maybe you need to take a break!

Elliot limped home that night going over all the things he had tried.

"Face it," he said to himself. "It's hopeless.
There's nothing you can do."

The next morning he said, out loud for everyone to hear, "I GIVE UP! I don't need anybody. I'm going to the forest where I can be alone and no one will ever find me!"

In the forest, Elliot found himself a quiet, grassy spot under a tree. He sat hugging his knees. "You give up what?" a little voice said. Elliot turned and saw another porcupine facing him.

"What's your name?" she asked.

"Elliot Kravitz," said Elliot Kravitz.

"I'm Thelma Claypits," said Thelma Claypits.

"What are you doing here?" she said.

"I'm here because nobody wants to hug me," said Elliot.

"I'll hug you," she said.

"You will?" said Elliot.

"Sure," said Thelma.

"But I'm a porcupine," said Elliot.
"What do you think I am?" she said, pointing
to her quills. "Let's hug."

And they tried *slowly* . . .

carefully...

very gently, they hugged.

Elliot smiled.

"This is nice," he thought to himself.